Did You Lose the Car

AGAIN?

Did You Lose the Car Again?

by Paula Kurzband Feder

and Nancy Hayashi

PUFFIN BOOKS

PUFFIN BOOKS
Published by the Penguin Group
Penguin Books USA Inc., 375 Hudson Street, New York, New York 10014, U.S.A.
Penguin Books Ltd, 27 Wrights Lane, London W8 5TZ, England
Penguin Books Australia Ltd, Ringwood, Victoria, Australia
Penguin Books Canada Ltd, 10 Alcorn Avenue, Toronto, Ontario, Canada M4V 3B2
Penguin Books (N.Z.) Ltd, 182–190 Wairau Road, Auckland 10, New Zealand

Penguin Books Ltd, Registered Offices: Harmondsworth, Middlesex, England

First published in the United States of America by Dutton Children's Books, 1990
Published in Puffin Books, 1991
10 9 8 7 6 5 4 3 2
Text copyright © Paula Kurzband Feder, 1990
Illustrations copyright © Nancy Hayashi, 1990
All rights reserved

Library of Congress Catalog Card Number: 91-52541
ISBN 0-14-034800-X

Speedsters is a trademark of Dutton Children's Books.

Printed in the United States of America
Set in Caledonia

to my parents,
Toby and Diana Kurzband

P. K. F.

for Brian and David

N. H.

ONE

"Where's my blue-and-yellow scarf?" yelled Dad from the bedroom.

"Karla," I said to my younger sister, "where's Dad's scarf?"

"I don't know, Phoebe," she said. "You wore it yesterday."

"Never mind," said Dad. "I'll just have
to wear your scarf, Phoebe, for our trip.
It's going to be cold in the country today."
"You're silly, Daddy," giggled Karla.

Dad grabbed Karla and held her up in the air. "I'm not silly," he said. "I need a scarf. And I know what else we need for our trip."

4

"No reading in the car," said Mom. She looked right at me.

"Oh, Mom," I said. "You're the only one who gets sick."

"No reading and no arguments, please," said Mom.

5

Then she turned to Dad. "Thomas, do you know where you parked the car this time?"

We knew Mom wasn't being silly. Dad really did lose the car once. He couldn't find a parking place near our house. He had to park the car so far away that he forgot where it was.

"I know where I parked it," he said. "Now everyone look for my scarf. I'll be back in ten minutes. Look at your watch, Phoebe. Ten minutes. Wait for me downstairs. Good-bye."

We looked for Dad's scarf. But we couldn't find it anywhere.

Then we went downstairs carrying crackers, a thermos of hot chocolate and extra scarves. I had a book in my coat pocket that Mom didn't see me take.

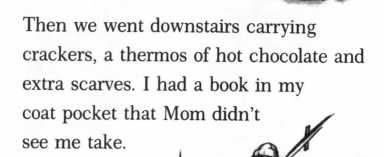

We waited ten minutes for Dad.

But we didn't see our car. It's light gray with black seats, and it's not very clean. A bumper sticker on the back says

"No it's not," said Mom. "Here comes Daddy, and he's not driving."

"Oh, Mom. He's walking," I said. "He lost the car."

AGAIN!

"Maybe someone stole it," said Karla.

"No one stole it," said Mom. She was angry.

That does it, Thomas. We sell the car, after we find it.

"How will we get to the country?"
I cried.

Mom looked at me. "We can take the
train or the bus to the country from now
on. And that is that."

"Let's all look for the car," said Dad.

"Let Karla and me look by ourselves," I said. "Please? We can walk up to 86th Street."

"That's a good idea," said Mom. "Dad and I can walk down to 79th Street."

I looked at my watch. "I heard you, Dad," I said. "Come on, Karla. Let's go."

"Be careful. And look both ways crossing the street. And stay together," said Mom.

"We know, Mom," I said.

"I'll find the car first," said Karla. "I have better eyes than you."

She skipped ahead of me.

14

TWO

We walked to 84th Street.
Suddenly Karla yelled, "There it is!"

She ran across the street.
A car was coming. The
driver slowed down.

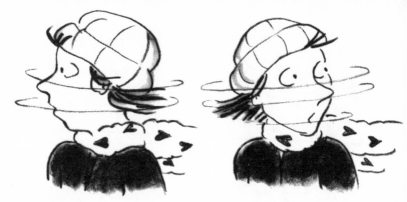

I looked both ways. Then I crossed the street and grabbed her.

"That was a stupid thing to do, Karla. You know you're not supposed to cross the street without me. And that car doesn't even look like ours."

I was very angry.

I'm sorry. I just wanted to find Daddy's car.

She took my hand.

We saw another gray car ahead, so Karla and I walked over. It wasn't ours. The seats were red, and it looked very bright and new.

"It's so shiny," said Karla. She reached out to touch it.

Suddenly the door opened. A woman got out of the car. She spoke in a loud voice.

Karla and I jumped.

Then she said, "All children have sticky fingers, and my car is brand-new. Stay away."

The woman just stared at us.

"I have gloves on," said Karla. "I don't have sticky fingers."

She was holding my hand tight. I shook it hard and she let go. She was hurting my fingers.

We walked away very fast. The woman
called after us. Then we began to run.

THREE

We ran to the drugstore
on 85th Street.

"We should keep looking for Daddy's car," I said to Karla.

"Maybe someone really *did* steal it, Phoebe. Maybe we should call the police."

"No. That's dumb. I'm hungry. Let's get something to eat in the drugstore. Then we can look some more."

Karla pulled on my hand. "I have to go to the bathroom, and I'm tired. I want to go home."

"Not yet," I said. "Let me see what time it is." I took off my glove to look at my watch.

It was gone.

I had lost my watch!

I looked at my
other hand,
just in case.

I looked in
my pockets.

I looked
in my shoes.

It wasn't anywhere.

"I lost my watch, Karla. What am I going to do?"

"Let's go home," said Karla.

"No. Let's go into the drugstore and find out what time it is."

But I forgot all about my watch. Just then, I saw a gray car with red seats coming up the street.

I grabbed Karla's arm.

Karla took my hand. We ran to the end of the block.

"She can't come this way," I said. "It's a one-way street, and it's the wrong way for her."

Just then, a bus came by and stopped.

I pulled Karla up
the steps and put two
tokens in the box.

Karla looked like
she was going to cry.
"We're late," she said. "And this bus isn't
going the right way. It's going away from
our house."

Eight blocks went by. We came to 93rd Street.

Then I saw it. I saw our car. There was the bumper sticker on the back and the black seats.

"Karla. Push the button, quick. I saw
our car. Hurry. We have to get off."

When the bus stopped, we got off and
ran down the block.

"Uh-oh, Karla. Look," I said. "It's got a parking ticket. Dad's not going to be happy about that."

"Are you really sure it's our car?" asked Karla.

I pressed my nose against the window and looked inside.

It's our car, Karla. Dad's blue-and-yellow scarf is on the floor.

FOUR

We started to run home. We were
twelve blocks away from our house. Even
without my watch, I knew we were going
to be late.

"Let me tell Mom and Dad about the car," I said. "I found it."

At a red light, we stopped running for a minute. We were out of breath.

Just a few more blocks.

Suddenly Karla shouted, "Phoebe, Phoebe! There she is. The witch!"

I looked where Karla was pointing. The gray car with the red seats was moving slowly down the side street. The witchy lady was inside.

I looked at the light. It was green, and we ran.

I could hear the lady shouting, "Children, stop. Stop right now."

At that moment, two things happened.
We saw Mom and Dad, and the witchy
lady stopped her car and got out.

Karla ran right into Mom. She almost knocked her down.

"Mommy! Daddy!" cried Karla. "She's following us."

"Well, for goodness sake," the woman
said. "You children are hard to catch
up to."

Then she looked right at me.

"I have something you lost, young lady,"
she said.

The woman was holding my watch.

"You lost your watch and you tried to lose me, but it didn't work. Now here's your watch, and I'll go."

"What is this all about?" asked Dad as we watched her walk to her car.

I didn't know how to begin, so Karla started talking. She forgot about being scared and began to jump up and down.

I gave Karla a poke.

47

I looked at them. "I saw it first, and we got off the bus, and . . ."

"What were you doing on the bus?" interrupted Dad.

"Let her finish, Thomas," said Mom.

"We got off the bus.
And we ran to the car.

It was our car.

And your blue-and-yellow scarf
was in there, Dad."

"Now calm down," he
said, "and tell us where
you saw the car."
"We saw it on
93rd Street," I said.

"And you got
a ticket, too," she
sang to him.

FIVE

We went home, and Karla got the bathroom first. I told Dad about the witchy lady.

"I'm glad she found your watch, Phoebe," he said. "She was a good witch, and she was right when she told you to stay away from other people's cars."

Then we gathered all our stuff and took a taxi to the car. Karla and I ate crackers in the taxi. We were hungry.

"There's the car!" shouted Karla. "There it is."

The taxi stopped. We got out, and Dad walked to the car. He took off the ticket.

"I will never forget again," he promised.

"You were lucky, Thomas," said Mom. "Our children have sharp eyes. If it wasn't for them, who knows what would have happened to our car."

I looked at Karla and smiled.

We drove out of the city at last.

Karla fell asleep. Mom poured hot
chocolate and gave some to Dad and me.

I took my book out of my coat pocket
and read all the way to the country.

This time Mom didn't seem to mind at all.